Theophilus Parvin

Philosophical problems in medicine: presidential address before the American Medical Association, at its thirtieth annual session, Atlanta, Ga., May 6, 1879

Antigonos

Theophilus Parvin

Philosophical problems in medicine: presidential address before the American Medical Association, at its thirtieth annual session, Atlanta, Ga., May 6, 1879

Reprint of the original, first published in 1879.

1st Edition 2024 | ISBN: 978-3-38801-255-1

Antigonos Verlag is an imprint of Outlook Verlagsgesellschaft mbH.

Verlag (Publisher): Outlook Verlag GmbH, Zeilweg 44, 60439 Frankfurt, Deutschland, info@outlook-verlag.de
Vertretungsberechtigt (Authorized to represent): E. Roepke, Zeilweg 44, 60439 Frankfurt, Deutschland
Druck (Print): Libri Plureos GmbH, Friedensallee 273, 22763 Hamburg, Deutschland

PRESIDENTIAL ADDRESS

BEFORE THE

AMERICAN MEDICAL ASSOCIATION,

AT ITS

THIRTIETH ANNUAL SESSION,

ATLANTA, GA., MAY 6, 1879.

BY

THEOPHILUS PARVIN, M.D.

EXTRACTED FROM THE
TRANSACTIONS OF THE AMERICAN MEDICAL ASSOCIATION.

PHILADELPHIA:
COLLINS, PRINTER, 705 JAYNE STREET.
1879.

PHILOSOPHICAL PROBLEMS IN MEDICINE.

PRESIDENTIAL ADDRESS

BEFORE THE

AMERICAN MEDICAL ASSOCIATION,

AT ITS

THIRTIETH ANNUAL SESSION,
ATLANTA, GA., May 6, 1879.

BY

THEOPHILUS PARVIN, M.D.

EXTRACTED FROM THE
TRANSACTIONS OF THE AMERICAN MEDICAL ASSOCIATION.

PHILADELPHIA:
COLLINS, PRINTER, 705 JAYNE STREET.
1879.

ADDRESS.

GENTLEMEN:—

SCIENCE, Literature, Philosophy, and Theology are the great subjects of human study. Science is the knowledge of nature and of nature's laws. Literature, including history,, is the representation of man's life; it tells his joys and sorrows, his aspirations and achievements, his victories and defeats, his glory and shame; it is "man's autobiography." Philosophy studies man's psychical nature, both in its mental and moral manifestations; it seeks to discover the relation he bears to the past and to the future, to nature and to the universe, and in its highest development brings the reflecting mind to believe in an ultimate unity, a great first cause, the fountain of all other causes, a power originant of them if not immanent in them. Theology discusses the being, attributes, and providence of the Divine, the uncreated, the eternal, whose existence philosophy in its sublimest aspirations maintains, even if that existence be not one of the fundamental convictions of the human mind.

Nevertheless, these divisions are in some degree arbitrary. For example, if there be a Divine Being, all-wise and all-powerful, and nature his creation, his name will be recorded on its pages; and to the study of such record, the title of natural theology has been given.

Moreover, man is a part of nature, made of the same material as countless other organisms, and subject to the same general laws, so that the science of physical man is a part of the science of nature. A complete knowledge of man, therefore, includes both science and philosophy.

That department of physical science which has for its objects the restoration from disease or injury, the preservation of human health and the prolongation of human life, is the queen of sciences, and in her royal right and in her grand work accepts the services of her handmaids, anatomy, physiology, chemistry, and botany, and commands the obedient subtle forces of nature.

And yet, if Medicine limits its knowledge to that of a mere machine, if its ultimate reason rests in the scalpel, retort, test-tube, and microscope, the whole of man's nature is not comprehended. Will, understanding, reason, conscience, are as surely a part of the human being as muscle and bone, nerve and vessel, liver and lung, brain and heart. Knowledge of the intellectual, of the emotive, and of the moral nature of man, of their laws and manifestations, is just as essential to the thoroughly furnished physician as any knowledge of the merely material organism.

With the marvellous advance made during recent years in some of the physical sciences, the light of their grand discoveries blazing about us, we are well-nigh blinded by the near and sudden glory, and some distant objects that we once saw distinctly, have altogether faded, or have grown so dim and shadowy that in "the strife of aching vision" we scarcely know what they are, where they are. Aristophanes, in one of his plays, ridiculing some of the philosophy of his day, taught that Vortex reigned in the place of Jupiter, and that the three gods in whom belief should be reposed were Chaos, the Clouds, and the Tongue. Twenty-three centuries had nearly passed and Comte found the Jupiter in man; the apotheosis of humanity was declared. Twenty-three centuries have passed, and in some of the literature of the day, philosophical and scientific, there might be found reason to repeat the very jest of the Greek poet.

The heavens here bright with new light; there dark with the disappearance of the old. We breathe an atmosphere of doubt—at any rate, of anxious inquiry—and sometimes find our footsteps tottering and uncertain.[1]* Nay, sometimes we seem wrapped in the thick darkness of conflicting opinions, and like Ajax in the long night of strife pray most earnestly for the light of day.

Science,[2] says one of its most distinguished American representatives, adopting the teaching of Lord Bacon, is the practical interrogation of nature. Let us interrogate medicine, discuss

---

* The numerals in the text refer to notes at the end of the Address.

some of its philosophical problems, and see if it makes any response to most earnest questionings of the human soul.

At the very outset of our inquiries is, Why does Medicine exist? What reason for it? It is born of human sympathy; it springs from the wants of man, and is an evidence of human power; it lives because it can live—it has a right to live. Montaigne wittily remarked that he rode his horse, not that he knew that he had any such right—possibly the horse had a right to ride him—but because the horse let him. Doctors, however, do not practise physic because the people let them, but because the people want them, demand them. Medicine comes in response to the cry of human suffering—of man's writhing with pain, or starting back, in instinctive horror, from imminent death.

Pain is the first lesson in the book of evil which most human beings, at one time or another of their lives, read in such bitterness of sorrow. "The idea of evil is a generalization from the perception of pain."[3]

And here we are brought face to face with this problem of physical suffering, this mystery of pain. "Pain expresses an ultimate fact of human consciousness, a primary experience of the human mind, resolvable into nothing more general or more fundamental than itself."[4] But why is this fact?

In reading John Stuart Mill,[5] one is almost tempted to believe that a worse than Nero is enthroned in nature, and is inflicting cruelties upon the human race, with less reason than the mistress in Juvenal chastised her slave.[6]

Herbert Spencer[7] rejects a Supreme Beneficence, because of the existence of suffering on the part of man and inferior creatures.

Among the reasons for the existence of pain, the most obvious is that which the word itself signifies. Often, indeed, pain is punitive. Tracing the word to its Greek[8] derivation, we find that it originally meant blood-money, or compensation for the killing of a kinsman, while the Latin *poena* simply expresses punishment.[9]

Undoubtedly, infractions of the laws of health or of virtue generally bring punishment, but not always or alone to the offender. Sometimes the wave of suffering widens, bearing innocent and guilty to a common ruin, or sweeps away only the innocent.

Countless children bear in their bones and written upon their faces, the sins, often of their fathers, sometimes of their mothers. Many a pure wife walks a *via dolorosa*, made for her by a licentious husband.

Pain is protective. This conservative power makes it one of the most efficient guardians of health.

The diagnostic value of pain is very great. Pain not only warns the patient of the approach or the presence of disease, but also guides the physician to its recognition and in its treatment.

There are moral uses of pain. Pain is a discipline: Jeremy Taylor has declared with his characteristic eloquence, "Softness is for slaves and beasts, for minstrels and useless persons, for such who cannot ascend higher than the state of a fair ox, or a servant entertained for vainer offices; but the man who designs his son for nobler employments, to honors and to triumphs, to consular dignities and presidencies of councils, loves to see him pale with study, panting with labor, hardened with sufferance, or eminent by dangers."

An attack of sickness may lead to an entire reformation of life. Then, too, what revelations of true nobleness, of all that is gentle and beautiful, unselfish and loving, have we witnessed on the part of some who were called to endure most painful, yea loathsome, yea hopeless disease; and we were ready to exclaim—

> "How sublime a thing it is to suffer and be strong."

The Prometheus Vinctus is one of the grandest ideals of ancient mythology.

One of the most distinguished of British scientific men, Prof. Owen, has admirably[10] depicted the beneficial subjective influence of suffering.

So, too, in the sympathy that human suffering evokes, the skill, the kindness, the self-sacrifice, and the unwearied, ever-watchful attention manifested for its relief, we see beneficial results. Take away, for example, those religious orders of women whose whole lives are consecrated to the care of the sick, women in regard to many a one of whom we might apply the words of Tennyson—

> "Her eyes are homes of silent prayer,
> Her loves in higher love endure"—

and one of the brightest pages of human history is blotted out. Thus, too, of all other noble, self-sacrificing remedial agencies for the sick.

What divine beauty of life, making sunshine in a shady place, is manifested by wife or mother, sister or daughter, when the home is entered by disease. There is no gloom of suffering too dark for woman's smile not to lessen, no depth of distress too profound for woman's sympathy and helpful hand not to reach.

Mr. Mill thinks it quite a natural question, Whether so complicated a machine as the human body could not have been made to last longer, and not get so easily out of order? Reference will be made to the first part of the question hereafter, and the answer that most physicians would make to the second part would be, that considering the needless wear and tear, and the general ill-usage, either from ignorance or neglect, these bodies get, it is wonderful they are not oftener out of order. Moreover, the experience of the vast majority of human beings testifies that so far as physical suffering is concerned, the good greatly overbalances the evil; days of health have been much more frequent than days of sickness.

Even with the various utilities of pain, both direct and indirect, that have been mentioned, we still must refer to it as often a mystery; much is revealed, but much else is hidden. The different attempted solutions of this remaining mystery we omit, only quoting in concluding the topic the eloquent words, in reference to it, of a distinguished London surgeon, the late Mr. Hinton.[11] "A touch might transform it wholly. One flash of light from the Unseen, one word spoken by God, might suffice to make the dark places bright, and wrap the sorrow-stricken heart of man in the wonder of an unutterable glory."

And yet one thought more. Mr. Jevons,[12] at the close of a paragraph referring to the presence of pain, and the difficult reconciliation of the fact with the hypothesis of a creator all-powerful and all-benevolent, remarks: "We perpetually find ourselves in the position of finite minds attempting infinite problems, and can we be sure that where we see contradiction an infinite intelligence might not discover perfect logical harmony?"

A similar view is found in these words of one of the most gifted poets of the century, Mrs. Browning:—

> "Experience, like a pale musician, holds
> A dulcimer of patience in his hand;
> Whence harmonies we cannot understand
> Of God's will in the worlds, the strain unfolds
> In sad, perplexed minors.
> We murmur, 'Where is any certain tune
> Of measured music in such notes as these?'
> But angels leaning from their golden seats
> Are not so minded. Their fine ear hath one
> The issue of completed cadences."

Greater than the mystery of life, it has been well said, is the mystery of death to child and savage. Nay, it is one of the greatest of mysteries unto all. But death is the law of all earthly existence. Lord Bacon has said that possibly it is as easy to die as to be born; certainly it is as natural; death is the necessary sequence of life—sequence, not consequence, for not death, but the continuance, the perpetuation of life is the purpose, the end of life. "The individual life is the continuation of anterior, and the fountain of ulterior lives."

Stahl, in the extraordinary powers with which he invested the Anima, making it the ruler and the governor of the body, has asked, "Since men can live for a time, why not always?"

While medicine has done much, and will do more to prolong the average of human life, the perpetuation of the individual existence is as vain a hope as increasing the physical development to that of the fabled Titans.

Storms on sea and on land, war, famine, pestilence, earthquakes, fire and flood, and the various so-called accidents on ship and on shore, have hurried millions to untimely graves. Even if none of these cut short human life, diseases in numerous forms—coming to us from our ancestry, coming from without or developed from within, coming at every stage of life—bear to the great majority the accursed shears of Atropos, so that few live to reach the goal of old age "weary, wayworn, and broken with the storms of life." Fontenelle, dying at ninety-nine years, when asked what he experienced, replied, simply the difficulty of existing.

To those who have thus had their days prolonged, death is inevitable from changes in the organism, degeneration of tissue rendering the performance of life's functions impossible.

It were a grievous thing if old men did not die, says Dr. Maudsley, for in that sad case the world's movement onward to where it is going would be very sluggish if it were not actually arrested. So, too, human longevity would violate that proportion established between the different stages of life in all the mammalia, or by the prolongation of the earlier stages in man would bring increased cares, casualties and liabilities to disease and death. It is not difficult, as Dr. Symonds has stated, to discover in the limitation of our existence its fitness to our constitution, **and to the universal frame of things.**

Life is sufficient for all its purposes if well employed, was the just observation of Dr. Johnson, "and what follower of medicine can forget that the immortal sage of Cos, by the example which he afforded in his well-spent life, disarmed his own antithesis of its woeful point," ο βίος βραχυς η δε τεχνη μάχρη.[13]

But what is this man thus made subject to disease and death, man whose *Misereres* are the invocation of the physician, and whose most grateful *Te Deums* ascend when the physician's skill **has restored health or rescued life?**

If, to the poets,[14] "one impulse from a vernal wood" has an important lesson "of moral evil and of good"—and the[15] "flower in the crannied wall" has the secret of man and of God—how much clearer revelation of high truths the proper study of man **might make to physicians.**

Consider the very commencement of human life in the fecundated ovum. Behold a cell $\frac{1}{120}$ of an inch in diameter, an ovum which neither chemistry nor the microscope can distinguish from the common mammalian ovum. And yet, in that human ovum there dwell physical potentialities, species, race, family, individuality; in that ovum there is the assured promise of all organs that, in their harmony and co-ordination, make a perfect organism. In every living germ, said the great French physiologist, Claude Bernard, there is a directing idea which is developed and manifested by the organization. One by whom some of us were instructed in our student days, the late Dr. Samuel Jackson, of the University of Pennsylvania, in[16] eloquent terms, declared that the ideal plan of the universe, in the minute as in the vast, for each individual as for the whole, must have preëxisted to the creation in the Divine mind. Does not this correspond with the teaching of Plato who made the causes of things an efficient architect, ideas and matter? But before Plato, the voice of one of earth's most famous kings bowing before the throne of the Author of existence, declared, "My substance was not hid from thee, when I was made in secret, and curiously wrought in the lowest parts of the earth. Thine eyes did see my substance, yet being imperfect; and in thy book all my members were written, which, in continuance, were **fashioned, when as yet there was none of them.**"

The facts of heredity are equally inexplicable, without the recognition of "a casual incarnation in the germ," of a directing idea making itself manifest through matter. Physical and chemical forces, molecular play of organic matter cannot explain the transmission of physical, intellectual, and moral qualities from parent to child; they cannot explain the slumbering, it may be through one or more generations, of these distinctive qualities, to reappear in subsequent ones. They are dumb before what has been termed the heredity of influence.[17]

It is remarkable, too, in the study of heredity[18] that moral qualities are transmitted with more certainty than intellectual.

Pathological heredity presents facts of the greatest interest. Thus we find disease transmitted from one or the other parent to the offspring, and this disease may show itself in the child before it does in the father or the mother. In illustration, a daughter dies of cancer, and subsequently the mother dies of cancer affecting the same or another organ. Or, again: the malady may date back to a grandparent, a father or mother giving to children that of which he or she presented not the **slightest manifestation during a long life.**

Then, too, one of the most surprising facts is pointed out by Prof. Chauffard, that of all the maladies which proceed from immediate progenitors, or having affected anterior generations, may be transmitted by a second generation, those which are the most certain of continuance, the most inevitable, are not those involving structural changes, not cancer or tubercle for example, but the *neuroses*, such as hysteria and epilepsy, diseases that present no appreciable organic alteration. What can chemistry say before such facts, and do they not testify that the most material element is lost in these transmissions, the more the directing **and final idea prevails?**

I will not wait to speak of the evolution of the various parts of the organism—of the swift and perfect formation of a brain where no thought can yet dwell—of the eye constructed where there is no light—of the ear where there is no sound, and of lungs where pulmonary respiration is impossible; all these and more marvels of ingenious and harmonious construction accomplished in a few months by the power of a single cell and from a single fluid. I speak not of the wonderful accommodation and adaptation on the part of the maternal organism for its high office—adaptation and accommodation so wonderful, indeed, that the[19] greatest of living obstetricians has spoken of them as a miracle.

Nor shall I speak of the transition to the external world, save to remind you that one of our own guild, one who, though dead for more than a century, is never mentioned without profound respect by both physicians and philosophers, Dr. David Hartley,[20] presents from this transition an ingenious argument for our immortality, the conclusion of the argument being that our birth was even intended to intimate to us a future life as well as to introduce us to the present.

Nor is it necessary for our present purpose to wander in the shades of speculation as to when, where, and how man originated. It matters not just now as to whether his was a special creation, or whether he is a descendant through uncounted millions of years of ascidian ancestry; whether the beginnings of life on our globe were from a single germ, from few or many germs, and whether those germs were placed here directly by a divine hand, or dropped from some star in its swift flight. Nay, even whether matter in the far-distant morning of the earth had " the promise and potency of every form and quality of life," an abiogenesis then possible of which no shadow of manifestation is seen to-day. No difference as to man's origin, lowly or lofty, remote or near, but consider man as he now is, " the heir of all the ages," and what is his nature?

The general belief of mankind is that this nature is dual, and that belief is expressed by the terms body and mind. " The distinction between them is so obvious that it is recognized in every language; and the knowledge of it, therefore, precedes speculation, and is anterior to all science and philosophy; for language is the expression and record of the primitive observation and unprejudiced common sense of mankind."[21] In its general acceptance it has the same evidence as Cicero[22] gives for a law of nature.

A distinguished French member[23] of the profession refers to " the duality of man's nature so universally admitted since the school of Plato, so dogmatically consecrated by the fathers of the church under the title of *homo duplex*, and so judiciously expressed in our day by the spiritualist school under the double denominations of the physiological and psychological man." He proceeds to state that this belief is anterior to all social institutions, to all legislation; that it is naturally and constantly in the universal consciousness of peoples; and that human duality is not only a moral fact, but a physiological law, and in conformity with logical law.

The assertion of human duality includes two propositions:— First, man has a physical organization; and second, associated with this physical organization is mind; mind and body are man, at least the only man we now know.

Let us first consider man as a material organism. He is born, grows, attains his acme of development and physical vigor, declines, decays, dies. Have physical forces their periods of youth, of maturity, and of old age? Has inorganic matter any corresponding periods? During his life, as in its very beginning,[24] a creative power is constantly manifested. By a chemistry more subtle than inorganic nature exhibits, this power lifts lifeless matter to life, creates the living from the dead. If the chemist in his laboratory has produced certain materials contained in inorganic matter, such as taurine and urea, they are in the body products of alteration, of decomposition, ready to be returned to the inorganic world; he has never made, he never can make liver cells, brain cells, blood globules. I do not believe. therefore, the phenomena of living beings can all be referred to physico-chemical laws, but we must, with Dr. Beale,[25] "accept the idea of vital power as being super-physical," and with that idea its correlate, a living Creator of such power.

Such a Creator as Beale refers to is very different from the God-atom which Büchner declares, "the atom, or the smallest indivisible and fundamental part of matter, is the God to whom all existence, the lowest and the highest, is indebted for its being." But really more familiar names than that of Büchner are identified with almost as strange an hypothesis.[26] Prof. Chauffard, referring to the suggested "evolution of living protoplasm from not-living matter," and the subsequent transformations of this protoplasm into all the forms of life our earth presents, as "impossibilities," exclaims: "And it is in the name of these impossibilities that a science which claims to be altogether experimental and positive, wishes to impose a complete genesis of organized beings, and excludes from this genesis all directing and final idea."

Of the perfections of the human body and its various organs, of the eye for example, so wonderful in construction and adaptation that the greatest of England's natural philosophers, Sir Isaac Newton, asked, "Did not He who made the eye know the laws of optics?" I shall not now speak. To believe that stones, responsive to the lyre of Amphion, took their places in symmetrical order and formed the walls of hundred-gated Thebes, or that the accidental association of letters constructed the Iliad, would be trifling trials to ordinary faith in comparison with believing that this human body, fearfully and wonderfully made, is not the work of intelligent design.[27]

I pass now to the consideration of the second proposition, to wit, the complete conception of man includes mind. Many years ago one of the most eminent of Scotch metaphysicians, the late Sir William Hamilton, said: "Should physiology ever succeed in reducing the facts of intelligence to the phenomena of matter, philosophy would be subverted in the subversion of its three great objects—God, free will, and immortality."

Has physiology reduced the facts of intelligence to the phenomena of matter? Certain utterances would seem to indicate that some answer this question affirmatively, and they believe the "soul is but the sum of the brain functions, and psychology but a chapter of physiology." "The brain secretes thought as the liver does bile." (Cabanis.) "—The view entertained by the best cerebral physiologists is, that the mind is a force developed by the action of the brain." (Hammond.) "Thought is a motion of matter." (Moleschott.)

Next we ascend to higher authorities, whose utterances are not quite so positive: "All states of consciousness in us are immediately caused by molecular changes of the brain substance." (Huxley.) "Subjective and objective faces of the same fact." (Herbert Spencer.) And then the "undivided twins" of Professor Bain, "mental and physical proceed together."

"The late Mr. Lewes argued that since feeling, or sensibility, is an invariable accompaniment of the action of nervous centres, it is more philosophical to regard the psychical and physical events as two parts of one reality, and consequently to view feeling as a co-efficient, and not, with Professor Huxley, as a collateral result of nervous process."[28]

Again, we learn from Professor Huxley: "In itself it is of little moment whether we express the phenomena of matter in terms of spirit, or the phenomena of spirit in terms of matter; matter may be regarded as a form of thought; thought may be regarded as a property of matter."[29]

Dr. Holmes wittily remarks that Professor Huxley gives bioplasm all that it can bear; from the quotations that I have made, some of us will think that matter is given a good deal more than it can bear.

Every one who has speculated upon the relations of the material to the immaterial, of body to mind, must be conscious of the great difficulties which beset the subject, of the clouds that surround him at almost every step. The results obtained, the conclusions reached by some whose opinions I have quoted, men whose abilities and fame are so great, surely do not commend themselves to most minds as ultimate truths. Nay, I think some of them are open to criticism, if not unequivocal rejection. Very wisely has one of the ablest philosophic thinkers[30] of the century observed: "Every one knows that in this dark and cloudy region, which intervenes between the two territories of mind and matter, we meet with some of the profoundest mysteries of our nature. Here we fall in with sleep, dotage, somnambulism, insanity—topics on which little or no light has been thrown. In the mists and clouds which forever brood over this dark gulf, a thousand errors have been lurking. In this border territory there is a continual warfare going on."

I do not propose any extended remarks upon this topic, but shall present some difficulties which are obvious in all schemes of mental physiology, or efforts to interpret the phenomena of mind by physical facts.

Consciousness lies at[31] the foundation of all knowledge, and physiology ought to give us a definite location for this if it be a pure brain function. Now turn to Carpenter, Huxley, and Ferrier, and after reading their statements as to the matter, take a later writer, Hermann, and see how that which we supposed was knowledge is swept away. Really, we fear consciousness may yet be set wandering through the body in search of a home, very much as the soul[32] has:—

"It is also impossible to assign any individual spot in the cerebrum as the seat of consciousness, since cases are known, in connection with almost every part, in which, when that part was destroyed or wanting, consciousness still remained. Consciousness may still remain after the destruction of one hemisphere."

There are strong arguments to sustain the view that memory, termed by Hamilton the conservative faculty, depends upon material impressions made upon the brain. It is an old theory, but has been presented by Dr. Holmes,[33] of course in a most striking and beautiful garb. Without criticising this material view from a philosophic standpoint, it is enough to repeat the question, Who reads the record? Behind these brain-pages crowded with impressions, there must be an intelligence to read them, or else they are mute and meaningless as a volume of Milton or of Shakspeare would be to a tree or rock.

An argument for the materiality of the mind has been based upon the fact that an increased quantity of certain materials, urea is the most notable, is eliminated consequent upon mental exertion. Professor Chauffard states that a man in repose passes in twenty-four hours twenty grams .46 of urea; if in energetic muscular exertion twenty-two grams .60 in the same length of time, and finally after intellectual exertion twenty-three grams .88. That is, a great orator, a great poet or painter expends in the exercise of his mind a trifle over one gram more than the hod-carrier or stevedore in the exercise of his muscles. An immortal poem, or painting, or one of Professor Huxley's grand addresses to be had at the rate of fifteen grains of urea for **every twenty-four hours!**

In regard to the two-faced unity, the Siamese twins, objective and subjective faces of the same fact explaining the relations of mind and body, of the material and spiritual, to my thinking two things are brought together that are essentially disparate and incomparable. Movement and thought cannot be combined in a self-consistent scheme.

When the phenomena of spirit are to be expressed in terms of matter or the reverse, we shall not always have plain sailing. I turn to Haller, that illustrious man of our profession whose fame is for all ages, and I read in his work on Physiology: "For that the nature of the mind is different from that of the body, appears from numberless observations, more especially from those abstract ideas and affections of the mind which have no correspondence with the organs of sense, for what is the color of pride, or what the magnitude of envy?" And Fenelon has said, ask any sensible person if his thought is round or square, white or yellow, warm or cold, divisible into six or twelve pieces, and he will laugh at you.

I think it will be difficult to persuade physicians who have directed their attention to what are called mental influences in the causation, in the aggravation and in the cure of disease, that there is not something in the human body superior to that body. Jolly[31] has given a most interesting lecture upon the "Will considered as a Moral Power and as a Therapeutic Means," in which he adduces cases of muscular paralysis, of convulsive cough, stammering, hysteria, chorea, nystagmus, and one of traumatic tetanus—the last being under the care of Cruveilhier—cases, many of which had been previously treated unsuccessfully by all the ordinary therapeutic means, and which were cured by the exercise of the will.

Sir Benjamin Brodie[35] narrates a striking instance of the sense of duty triumphing over pain. Every physician can recall similar instances occurring under his own observation.

I have not time to continue the discussion of this topic, and yet let me quote the utterances of two eminent men in our profession—the one still living, the other deceased a few years ago. The late Sir Henry Holland observed: "I will merely remark, in correction of a common misapprehension, that the further we proceed in unravelling the brain as a collection of nervous fibres, condensed into separate organs for the establishment of their several functions and relations, the more in fact do we detach the mind itself from all material organization." Guenéau de Mussy exclaims: "Combine together oxygen, carbon, hydrogen, nitrogen, phosphorus, as much as you will, and you can make nothing which will be the representative or equivalent of intellectual or moral acts."[36]

We may weigh the brain, count its billions of cells, measure the rate of sensory impressions or motor impulses, localize cerebral functions, analyze cerebral matter; but after all possible observations, calculations, and analyses, it will always be inconceivable[37] that a displacement of molecules, or an undulation, or a vibration, or any mechanical or chemical phenomenon whatever, may be, not the condition of thought, but thought itself. The identity of corporeal and of spiritual phenomena is an affirmation which ought to be consigned to the list of impossible hypotheses.[38]

Is not the scientist of to-day who explains mental phenomena by mechanical or chemical changes, simply following in the footsteps of the old chemists, who found an explanation for all the mysteries of nature, and even of religion, in salt, **sulphur, and mercury?**

Physical science cannot express nor explain the mental and moral qualities of man: we cannot conceive that conscience, reason, joy and sorrow, are mere modifications of gray cerebral matter. The common sense of mankind will forever revolt against attributing to such modifications the profound thoughts of Plato, the winged words of Homer, the virtue of Socrates, the eloquence of Demosthenes, the philanthropy of Howard, the inspirations of a Mozart, the sublime conceptions of a Raphael, the faith of the martyr, and the love of the mother.

The problem of Teleology[39] commends itself especially to our profession. Even though human beings are but conscious automata, as there is a design, a purpose, and end for which every machine is constructed, so there must be a design in our bodies. The doctrine of automatism is, according to the late Mr. Lewes, the reflex theory legitimately carried out. That theory is used by Hermann[40] to explain volition, and indeed by others has been made to support the physical basis of mind. To the medical man an argument against the extension given this theory is found in pathology, but its presentation would divert me from my present purpose. It is enough to repeat that human automatism does not materially invalidate teleology.

Neither is the doctrine of final causes destroyed if it gives no explication of all facts and events. Non-recognition of this truth, it seems to me, is an error into which one of our most eminent scientific men has recently fallen.[41] " Just so far," says Professor Newcomb, " as the theologian can reconcile the motions of the planet or the burning of the theatre with final causes, or with a directing hand, so far is he at liberty to reconcile the whole course of nature in the same way." The assertion has been previously made that " the theory of final cause assumes that things have been arranged with a visible purpose."[42] But when we remember, as taught by Mr. Jevons, that there is probably no science entirely free from empirical and unexplained facts; and when he further states that logic approaches most nearly this position, but is not free from such facts, the teleologist may easily justify his position in cases of unexplained facts. Because a certain person reasonably skilled in arithmetic cannot solve two selected arithmetical problems, no one would be justified in concluding there is no such science as arithmetic. Furthermore,[43] those who maintain that there are final causes in nature are not thereby bound to maintain that there are only such, and that they must always and everywhere prevail over efficient causes.

Teleology is not set aside by the development theory. This theory, finding such strong support in embryology and in palæontology, and accepted, probably by three-fourths of scientific men, although they cannot admit the adequacy[44] of the causes of evolution advanced by its chief expounder, Mr. Darwin, is not antagonistic to the doctrine of final causes, "and even on the contrary naturally appeals to it, or else the theory of evolution is only the theory of chance under a more learned name"

The truth is, if you deny intelligent design in nature you cannot predicate it of man's works. If the blind stream of physical causation explains the vast and varied phenomena of earth's countless organisms, animal and vegetal, then the acts and works of men are similarly produced. Honor no more the skilful engineer or architect; no more crown the hero with laurels, or gratefully praise the poet, the painter, the philanthropist. All splendid human achievements and noble works are merely reflex phenomena. So, too, burn your scaffolds and tear down your penitentiaries. Individuals are as irresponsible for their actions as the falling stone, the rushing river, the sunshine or the storm.[45]

Nor is teleology to be rejected because of its abuses. Voltaire, who presents an argument[46] for the doctrine worth any man's reading, refers to some of these abuses,[47] and while condemning them, defines a final cause as one that acts at all times and in all places. He further declares that one must close his eyes and understanding who pretends there is no design in nature; and if there be a design there must be an an intelligent cause; God is.[48]

Time is wanting to present any of the striking evidences of design offered by the human[49] body, offered in its anatomy, in its physiology and its pathology. Nor is it necessary, for every physician knows them. Mr. Darwin, whose long devotion to scientific pursuits is so well known, and whose various and extensive observations of nature are so admirable, in referring to certain plants, observes that "the contrivances and adaptations transcend in an incomparable degree the contrivances and adaptations which the most fertile imagination of the most imaginative man could suggest, with unlimited time at his disposal." How much more, then, will the physician in the study of physical man find admirable contrivances and adaptations. And thus we are inevitably led to see the force of Voltaire's argument.

We read in Hippocrates that Medicine is full of reverence for the gods. And again, after most eloquently referring to the changes in nature, alternations of seasons, of day and night, the actions and experiences of individuals, the Father of Medicine declares that everything is accomplished by reason of divine necessity, δι' αναγχην θειην.

Once more the voice of Galen, meditating upon the structure and functions of the body, is heard: "Compono hic profecto Canticum in Creatoris nostri laudem." Again Sir Thomas Browne speaks: "In our study of anatomy there is a mass of mysterious philosophy, and such as reduced the very heathens to divinity." And then from the same century, prolific of great men, comes the vision of one not so famous in literature as Sir Thomas, but immortal in science—one contemporary with Lord Bacon, and his physician, and who doubtless knew all the great philosopher's censures of the impertinence of final causes in physics, while holding those causes were properly "inquired in metaphysique." The vision is of William Harvey, small of stature, with his keen, black eyes, his olive complexion, and his long hair, changed in old age from the color of the raven's wing to that of snow. Listen to his words in defence of his study of the lower animals: "If you will enter with Heraclitus in Aristotle into a workhouse (for so I call it), for inspection of viler creatures, come hither, for the immortal gods are here likewise; and the great and Almighty Father is sometimes most conspicuous in the least and most inconsiderable creatures." And again, as he studies embryology in the hatching of a chicken: "There inheres in some way or other, in every efficient cause a *ratio finis* (a final cause), and by this the efficient co-operation with Providence is moved."

And what shall be said of his great discovery? It was made under the inspiration of teleology, and using his reason aright. Harvey, says Professor Ackland,[50] believing in God, believed that there is purpose as well as harmony in the material world. He acted in this faith and, using his reason aright, he made a mighty discovery, which has influenced every biological student to this day, and will influence them to the end of time.

David Hartley tells us that "final causes,[51] *i. e.*, natural good, are the best clew for guiding the invention in all attempts to **explain the œconomy of animals.**"

Sir Charles Bell, rising from his famous researches in the nervous system, as if with oath-like solemnity, lifts up the Human Hand an ever-present, everlasting testimony unto man of Divine **Power, Wisdom, and Goodness.**[52]

Could array of grander witnesses and of more conclusive testimony be adduced to prove medical faith in the doctrine of final causes? Are there occasionally those who deny this faith or doubt this creed? That distinguished surgeon of Strasburg, Sédillot, has said: "Some[53] physicians, carried away by convictions more impassioned than wise, have found it possible, at rare intervals and in moments of forgetfulness, to doubt the existence of one Supreme Cause, but their vain efforts at revolt against the universal conscience remain without echo and without influence upon science."

[51]Sir Henry Holland and Dr. Prichard have each borne unequivocal testimony to their belief in the existence of the Supreme Being.

Professor Tyndall exclaims: Whence come we; whither go we? The question dies without an answer—*without an echo*—upon the infinite shores of the unknown. How the utterance of this great scientific teacher, utterance bearing most mournful truth, so far as science is concerned, seems almost like an echo through more than twelve centuries of the words of the aged Ealdorman to the King of Northumbria: "So seems the life of man, O King, as a sparrow's flight through the hall where you are sitting at meat in the wintertide, with the warm fire lighted on the hearth, but the icy rain-storm without. The sparrow flies in at one door, and tarries for a moment in the light and heat of the hearth-fire, and then, flying forth from the other, vanishes into the wintry darkness whence it came. So tarries for a moment the life of man in our sight; but what is before it, what after it, we know not." Human experience and human science are thus at one; known not and unknown are their final utterances.

But, on the other hand, is there from the study of man no light, though it be faint as the first tremblings of dawn upon black, mist hung waves? We have found in such study that man has a physical nature, in the commencement and continuance of which an idea dominated; that it was a continual creation; that there was an organic unity, and the constant mani festation of a power superior to physico-chemical forces.

Dwelling in this body is [55]mind, "in its perfection one and indivisible, in the image of its Creator,"[56] an immaterial, supra-natural element. Man[57] is the only one of all created beings to whom has been given the power of perceiving that he perceives, of thinking that he thinks, of knowing that he knows. There animates this machine a self-conscious and immortal principle, declares Professor Draper; and the eloquent words of Sir Thomas Browne will perpetually recur to the thoughtful mind: "There surely is a piece of divinity in us, something that was before the elements, and owes no homage to the sun." Answering to the vital unity of the body, we find a spiritual unity in the immaterial nature—physiology and psychology have corresponding truths.

Let this body be "blown about the desert dust, or sealed within the iron hills," it does not follow that the love and the hope, the aspiration and the desire, the knowledge, the will, the reason and the conscience—those spiritual elements which defy weights and measures, chemical analysis, and the most powerful objectives — should perish[58] with the material organization. Certain instincts were given for the preservation of the body, and they rarely deceive or betray their trust. So there are spiritual instincts which, in their up-springing, would seem to promise, as to the ancients the bursting pomegranate symbolized, immortality.

Add to these considerations those which flow from our belief in a Supreme Power, wise and benevolent, as suggested by a study of final causes, and there is something more than an echo from the shores of the unknown. We cannot, we cannot yet believe that man has

> —— "rolled the psalm to wintry skies,
> And built him fruitless fanes of prayer."

Since we last met together, less than a year ago, hundreds of our profession have fallen victims to the pestilence that walked in darkness and wasted at noonday in so many of the cities of the South. Some of those who thus fell in their efforts to save their fellow beings from swift death, were in the meridian of their powers and professional success. Others were in the fair morning, with the promise of long years and the hope of high honors. Can we believe that these heroic men live[59] only in the memory of their friends? From all the martyr-memories of noble men and women in every age, who counted not their lives dear unto them when principle was at stake, or in sublime self-abnegation sacrificed those lives for kindred, for country, for humanity, there comes a solemn protest against denial of life **beyond the grave.**

Accepting gratefully all the facts of science, let us beware of rejecting[60] everything that may not be capable of mathematical demonstration, and compelling our assent by absolute necessity. There may be truths more important, but less open; whisperings of hope that are sure promises of fruition. The poet tells of the sea-shell when shaken and its polished lips applied to **your attentive ear,**

> "And it remembers its august abodes,
> And murmurs as the ocean murmured there."

So if we listen, we may hear the deep but distant murmur of the immortal sea as it beats against the shores of time, ready to bear upon its mighty bosom the children of men from life to life, and the law of Continuity be found as true of the spiritual as it **is of the material world.**

Happy for us, though, unlike the Thracians, we hold no festivities over the dead, if with something of the glad dream of hope, if not in the glory of triumph, we can adopt the familiar **words of our great American poet :—**

> "There is no death ! what seems so is transition ;
> This life of mortal breath
> Is but a suburb of the life Elysian,
> Whose portal we call death."

NOTES.

1. Page 92, Line 32.

Stirling, in one of his annotations (translation of Schwegler), remarks that the heresy of the German critics is, perhaps, quite as active in England at present as the positivism of Comte; and further utters the warning exclamation, "Truly, we are on the brink of the most fearful crisis in the world's history."

2. Page 92, Line 36.
Dr. Draper.

3. Page 93, Line 18.
Baring-Gould.

4. Page 93, Line 23.
Alexander Bain.

5. Page 93, Line 24.

See his essay upon "Nature." Take the following extract as a part of the terrible indictment: "In the clumsy provision which she has made for that perpetual renewal of animal life, rendered necessary by the prompt termination she puts to it in every individual instance, no human being ever comes into the world, but another human being is literally stretched on the rack for hours or days, not unfrequently issuing in death."

Physicians know that labor in the vast majority of cases of healthy women, rarely lasts more than a few hours; and that in almost every instance the suffering attendant upon it may be greatly mitigated, sometimes entirely abolished, by the judicious use of an anæsthetic. They know, too, that the mortality, especially the maternal mortality, is very small, and no intelligent obstetrician would say that the mechanism of parturition is clumsy.

6. Page 93, Line 27.
Sic volo, sic jubeo; stat pro ratione voluntas.

7. Page 93, Line 28.

"With the conception of two antagonistic powers, which severally work good and evil in the world, the facts are congruous enough. But with the conception of a Supreme Beneficence, this gratuitous infliction of misery on man, in common with all other terrestrial animals capable of feeling, is absolutely incompatible."—*Biology.* If permitted to criticize the language of such a master as Herbert Spencer, I would ask, How can there be misery to animals unless they are capable of feeling?

8. Page 93, Line 33.

Wedgewood's "Dictionary of English Etymology."

9. Page 93, Line 36.

Dean Trench, "Study of Words," remarks that some "would fain have us to believe that pain is only a subordinate kind of pleasure, or, at most, a sort of a needful hedge and guardian of pleasure. But a deeper feeling in the universal heart of man bears quite another explanation of the existence of pain in the present economy of the world, namely, that it is the correlative of sin, that it is punishment; and to this the word pain, so clearly connected with 'pœna,' bears witness. Pain is punishment, for so the word and so the conscience of every one that is suffering declares."

10. Page 94, Line 30.

"Patience, endurance, faith in the end designed, a nature purified as by fire, accepting the trial with thanksgiving,—these be facts visible amongst the highest recognizable phenomena offered to our ponderings here below.

"Whoso has looked upon one so proved slowly consuming, with the inevitable grave in view, may have beheld, as it were, the face of an angel, have found the fitting expression for the visible radiance from that suffering body in Paul's temple of the holy one, have received conviction that in such sufferer was happiness ineffable, such as no mundane prosperity could yield, transcending any felt by an emperor in the highest pride of place, the welcomer of kings and kaisers honoring him by visits; for with them a pale figure, with breast battered, blackened and imbrued, rises more tragically than Banquo's ghost to mar the climax.

"Some who may have lost a loved one by cancer, will know that I state a fact. We may accept it and go no further in thought; the evidence of the result being, however, as plain as the trial." (Extract from "Answer to Mr. Lewes's Argument of Infirmity in his Review of the Reign of Law." By Prof. Richard Owen. *Fraser's Magazine*, October, 1867.)

11. Page 95, Line 27.

"The Mystery of Pain." D. Appleton & Co., New York, 1872.

12. Page 95, Line 31.

Principles of Science.

13. Page 97, Line 13.

Had time permitted, it was my intention to include in this discussion a fuller reference to the miseries and to the mortality of man, briefly alluding in such connection to that philosophy with which the names of Schopenhauer and Hartmann are identified, *Pessimism*, of which Caro speaks* as *une sorte de maladie intellectuelle*. It was my wish to show that such philosophy—the last cry of insane and utter despair—has no adequate support in professional experience: doctors, though probably not optimists, are still very far from being pessimists.

---

* Le Pessimisme au XXXe Siecle. Paris, 1878.

Even from human misery, conclusions very opposite to those of Schopenhauer and Hartmann have been drawn. Bulwer has said the discontent of the mortal proves the immortal. And Pascal, thus all these miseries prove man's greatness. They are the miseries of a great lord, of a dethroned king.

When man, either from mental or physical pain, or from weariness of living, deliberately destroys his life, it has been interpreted as an indication of his superiority to animal creation. Bossuet has remarked that to determine deliberately, with clear knowledge and reason to die, notwithstanding all the disposition of the body opposes the design, marks a principle superior to the body ; and among animals man is the only one having this principle.

It was my hope also to refer to the remarkable discourse* of Dr. B. F. Cotting in which its distinguished author ably maintains the thesis, "*Disease is a Part of the Plan of Creation*, one of the myriad expressions of Divine thought." In this discourse Dr. Cotting brings out, with great distinctness, the fact that disease and death were in the earth long before the advent of man, and therefore the *moral* explanation of these conditions, an explanation founded upon a single human transgression, fails. It is doubtful whether many theologians of the present day regard this explanation as valid. I quote from an eloquent discourse by Canon Farrar the following passages : "Ages before the first man, the primeval monsters had torn each other in their slime. For long ages the world had been a theatre of conflict and carnage, of wounds and mutilation ; and naturalists tell us that no armory can compete for variety, for beauty, for polish, for sharpness, for strength, for barbed effectiveness, with the lethal weapons of the fossil world." . . . "Yet this death is but the least dreaded part of the other, that second, that spiritual death which God meant in that earliest warning, 'In the day that thou eatest thereof, dying thou shalt die.' "

14. PAGE 97, LINE 18.
Wordsworth.

15. PAGE 97, LINE 19.
Tennyson.

16. PAGE 97, LINE 34.

"If a piece of mechanism, an instrument, or any contrivance is met with, though the construction be unknown, no one doubts that it is the work of an intelligent being ; and further, that it must have existed as an ideal form in an intelligent mind before it could have acquired an actual form.

"If we would seek to inquire deeper into these phenomena, and the law that governs their production, it would be a vain effort. We have reached the limit of human research ; we touch the veil that hides the infinite from the finite, not to be raised by human hands.

"There is but one conclusion that can be adopted. The ideal plan of the universe, in the minute as in the vast, for each individual as for the whole, must have preëxisted to the creation in the divine mind. The creative idea of the ever-present, all pervading presence of God continues to reproduce and to maintain in existence all created forms, after their original types, by the instrumentality of the forces which God has spread throughout nature." (Dr. Samuel Jackson, Introductory Address, University of Pennsylvania, 1844.)

* Annual Discourse before the Massachusetts Medical Society, May 31, 1865.

17. PAGE 98, LINE 14.

A widow marries, and bears children presenting a striking resemblance to her first husband long since dead.

18. PAGE 98, LINE 15.

See article on Heredité by Aug. Voisin, Nouveau Dictionnaire de Médecine et de Chirurgie Pratiques. To the important statement in the text may be added that which Rush makes as to the moral powers being the last to fail in old age.

19. PAGE 99, LINE 6.
Dr. Robert Barnes.

20. PAGE 99, LINE 11.

"The pain which attends the child during its birth or passage into the world, the separation and death of the *placenta*, by which the child received its nourishment *in utero*, with other circumstances, resemble what happens at death. Since, therefore, the child, by reason of its birth, enters upon a new scene, has new senses, and by degrees, intellectual powers of perception conferred upon it, why may not something analogous to this happen at death? Our ignorance of the manner in which this is to be effected is certainly no presumption against it, as all who are aware of the great ignorance of man will readily allow. Could any being of equal understanding with man, but ignorant of what happens at birth, judge beforehand that birth was an introduction to a new life, unless he was previously informed of the suitableness of the bodily organs to the external world? Would he not rather conclude that the child must immediately expire upon so great a change, upon wanting so many things necessary to its existence and being exposed to so many hazards and impressions apparently unsuitable." Then follows the conclusion given in the text. ("Observations on Man," part second, page 386; first printed in 1749.)

21. PAGE 99, LINE 36.
Prof. Bowen, *Princeton Review*, March, 1878.

22. PAGE 99, LINE 37.

"Omni in re consensio omnium gentium lex naturæ putanda est. Opinionum enim commenta delet dies, naturæ judicia confirmat." (M. Tullius Cicero, Quæstiones Tuscalanæ, lib. I, c. 13.)

23. PAGE 99, LINE 39.
Jolly.

24. PAGE 100, LINE 17.

"Biology cannot be reduced to the pure mechanism of matter until it is shown that germs or seeds are simple aggregates, and that the phenomena of the formation of organisms, as well as those of generation, are of the same order as the phenomena of affinity and of cohesion." (Ernest Neville, *Revue Philosophique*, March, 1879.)

25. Page 100, Line 27.

"Now, he who accepts the idea of the existence of vital power as being super-physical, will almost necessarily be led to believe that the creator of such power has attributes infinitely transcending those which any supposed creator of the inorganic only would need. The creator of the living must be ever living, and must possess power to form, guide, govern and vary, which would be useless to one who could create non living matter and its forces. In fact, if we admit that there are living things, still it is not possible to resist accepting the idea of the existence and constant superintendence of an all-powerful influence in nature, such as has been recognized in every age, and by nearly all people regarded as supernatural and distinguished as divine." (Beale.)

26. Page 100, Line 35.

"La Vie: Etudes et Problemes de Biologie Générale." Chauffard. Paris, 1878.

27. Page 101, Line 13.

I need not say that these illustrations are used by Fenelon—*De l'Existence de Dieu*. One of them, indeed, Fenelon had adapted from Cicero.

28. Page 101, Line 41.

Sully's "Pessimism," page 466, where a criticism is made of the *monism* of Mr. Lewes.

29. Page 102, Line 5.

This statement in reference to thought as a property of matter, is quite in contrast with the observation of Pascal: "La matière est dans une incapacité naturelle invincible de penser."

30. Page 102, Line 19.

President McCosh.

31. Page 102, Line 31.

"Whoso has mastered the elements of philosophy knows that the attributes of unquestionable certainty appertain only to the existence of a state of consciousness so long as it exists; all other beliefs are mere probabilities of a higher or lower order." (Professor Huxley.)

32. Page 102, Line 38.

The centre assigned the soul, according to Pythagoras, Plato, Cicero, and Galen, was the encephalon; Erasistratus, the meninges; Herophilus, the great ventricle; Servetus, the aqueduct of Sylvius; Arantius, the third ventricle; Des Cartes, the pineal gland; Sœmmering, the liquid contained in the encephalon; others, the origin of the spinal cord, the corpus callosum, the corpora striata, etc. Aristotle placed it in the heart, while Empedocles had it circulating in the blood. (Tissot—*La Vie dans l'Homme.*)

33. Page 103, Line 7.
Mechanism in Thought and Morals.

34. Page 104, Line 8.
Revue Médicale, 1875.

35. Page 104, Line 16.

"A barrister of my acquaintance, who afterward rose to the highest honors of his profession, was subject to a neuralgic disease, which so affected him that it often happened when he had to advocate an important cause that he entered the court in a state of most intense bodily suffering. But his sense of duty was greater than his sense of pain, and the latter was almost forgotten as long as the necessity for exertion lasted." (Brodie's "Psychological Inquiries.")

36. Page 104, Line 31.

I might add to these testimonies that of Sir Benjamin Brodie, as follows: "It is to me wholly inconceivable that any exaltation of the known properties of matter should produce the conscious indivisible monad which I feel myself to be When the materialist argues that we know nothing of mind except as being dependent on material organization, I turn his argument against himself, and say that the existence of my own mind is the only thing of which I have any positive and actual knowledge. I cannot help believing in an external world. Still the hypothesis of its non-existence implies no contradiction; whereas it is as much a contradiction to doubt the existence of my own mind as it would be to doubt that two and two are equal to four."

37. Page 104, Line 36.
Naville, op. cit.

38. Page 104, Line 41.

"The moral and intellectual faculties of man belong to a region for which physical science has no language and no explanation." (*Edinburgh Review.*)

39. Page 105, Line 16.

Mr. Mill, in his "System of Logic," remarks: "The word 'teleology' is also, but inconveniently and improperly, employed by some writers as a name for the attempt to explain the phenomena of the universe from final causes." This criticism seems to me incorrect, for the use condemned corresponds to the etymology of the word, and is consecrated both by time and the judgment of many of the most eminent philosophical writers.

40. Page 105, Line 22.

"Unless one is willing to admit the inadmissible assumption that processes which are not essentially movements of material particles, and the converse, we are compelled to surmise the existence of a connection between the nerve excitations connected with sensation and will, which is analogous to reflex actions." ("Physiology," by L. Hermann, translated by Mr. Gamgee. London, 1878.)

41. PAGE 105, LINE 32.

North American Review, May, 1879.

42. PAGE 105, LINE 39.

The purpose is not always visible, but is it generally visible?   Neither misconception nor misinterpretation disproves purpose.

43. PAGE 106, LINE 7.

Janet, "Final Causes."

44. PAGE 106, LINE 14.

Murphy, "Habit and Intelligence," second edition, London, 1879, page 375, observes: "We thus conclude that the time needed for the evolution of the highest forms of life out of the lowest would probably require, on the Darwinian theory, more than three thousand millions of years, while the entire duration of geological time cannot have been more than one-eighth of this."

45. PAGE 106, LINE 30.

The late Professor Herbert, in his work upon "Modern Realism," London, 1879, has ably presented the necessity for recognizing intelligence and purpose in nature, or else denying them to the works of man.

46. PAGE 106, LINE 32.

"Dictionnaire Philosophique."

47. PAGE 106, LINE 33.

Ridiculing these, Voltaire suggests that the nose was made to wear spectacles, the feet shoes.   Coleridge once said: "You abuse snuff.   Perhaps it is the final cause of the human nose."   Matthew Arnold, in one of his essays, in like manner remarks, the donkey exists that the invalid Christian may have milk.   But the abuses thus ridiculed may have a counterpart, thus, as a witty Frenchman has put it: "I have the toothache; therefore, there is no God."
I find in Dr. Maudsley's "Physiology of the Mind," page 147, the following: "M. Bert has made many extremely interesting experiments on grafting parts cut from the body of one animal on to that of another.   For example, he cut off the paw of one rat and grafted it in the flank of another rat; it took root there, and went through its normal growth, beginning to dwindle after a time. Where was the design of its going through its regular development there?   Or what, in the temporary adoption and nutrition of this useless member, was the final purpose of the so-called intelligent vital principle of the rat on which the graft was made?"   Readers of Vulpian's "Lectures, Phys. du Syst. Nerveux," need not be told that this objection is a repetition of the thought, almost of the words, of Vulpian, and that, as Jowet, referring to the statements of Vulpian, has said, it is directed against the doctrine of *the vital principle*, rather than against *final causes*.   Suppose the tail or paw of one rat transplanted to another rat does grow in its abnormal situation, grow uselessly and injuriously, must God make exceptions to a general law in order to guard against the cunning experiments of ingenious physiologists and the adroit arguments of not less ingenious logicians?

48. Page 106, Line 38.

I introduce the statements of Voltaire, partly to correct the notion that teleology belongs exclusively to theologians. It is a question for all intelligent persons, and a question of philosophy, not solely of theology. The scientist, because he does not use the doctrine in his methods, has therefore no right either to deny its reality, or to consign it to the sole custody of theologians.

49. Page 106, Line 40.

Even Mr. Mill remarks: "The human body, for example, is one of the most striking instances of artful and ingenious contrivances which nature offers."

50. Page 108, Line 3.

The Harveian Oration, 1865.

51. Page 108, Line 8.

Op. cit.

52. Page 108, Line 14.

The following passage from Sydenham is of interest in connection with this topic. I quote from page 76 of the translation of his work published in 1711: "In the last Place, I will add only this short Note, lest perchance any one should wrest my Opinion by a sinister Interpretation, or at least, not thoroughly understand it, *viz.* That in the preceding Discourse I often use the Word Nature, and attribute various Effects to her, as if I would represent under this Title some one thing subsisting of it self, and spread every where through the whole Machine of the World, which being endued with Reason, governs all Bodies, such a Thing as some of the Philosophers seemed to think was the Soul of the World. But as I do not affect novelty of Things, so neither of Words; and therefore I use in these Pages the ancient Word indeed, but in a sense, unless I am deceiv'd, both sober, and not only understood, but also used by the best Men; for as often as I mention Nature, I mean a certain complex of natural Causes, which are govern'd by the best Counsel in performing their Operations, and accomplishing their Effects, tho' they are without Reason, and destitute of all Skill, *viz.* supreme Deity, by whose Power all Things are produced, hath so disposed all Things by his infinite Wisdom, that they betake themselves to their appointed Functions, doing nothing that is vain, but that which is best and fittest for the whole Fabrick of Things, and their own private Nature, and so are moved like Engines, not by their own Skill, but by that of the Artificer."

The illustrious Boërhaave might be referred to as also believing in a Divine Order, yea in a Divine Providence. In his seventieth year, when in his last illness, which was both very painful and protracted, he wrote: "Patienter expectans Dei jussa, quibus resigno data; quae sola amo, et honoro unicè."

53. Page 108, Line 19.

Gazette Médicale de Strasbourg, 1855.

54. PAGE 108, LINE 25.

Sir Henry says : "The 'single' fact and 'great truth' is that of one Almighty cause, a conclusion to which we are irresistibly carried forward from every side ; surmounting in this inference those intermediate gradations of existence and power, which are too dimly seen to be rightly apprehended by the faculties of man in his present state of being."

"The whole universe displays the most striking proofs of the existence and operations of intellect or mind, in a state separate from organization, and under conditions which preclude all reference to organization. There is, therefore, at least one being or substance of that nature which we call mind separate from organized body, not only somewhere, but everywhere." (See introduction to Prichard on "Nervous Diseases.")

55. PAGE 109, LINE 12.

The following is an extract from the famous Hunterian oration of the late Mr. Lawrence:—

"Where shall we find proof of the mind's independence of the bodily structure? Of that mind which, like the corporeal frame, is infantile in the child, manly in the adult, sick and debilitated in disease, frenzied or melancholy in the madman, enfeebled in the decline of life, and annihilated by death."

In the last clause Mr. Lawrence assumed one of the points at issue between the materialist and the spiritualist. But it is impossible to prove the assumption, viz., the annihilation of the mind at death.

Futhermore, the spiritualist would answer that the immateriality of the mind is not necessarily disproved by its present dependence upon the bodily structure. It is quite rational that the child's mind, like the child's muscle, should be that of a child. The difference is vast between the locomotive of to-day and the locomotive first invented. Is the difference between the mind of the adult and that of the child any greater? The complete formation and the accurate working of all its parts, is essential in every machine, complex or simple, in order that human intelligence may obtain from it its best results. And so of the instrument which the mind uses. Not even a Mozart could evoke music from untuned cords. Let the brain be disordered,

> "Now see that noble and most sovereign reason,
> Like sweet bells jangled, out of tune and harsh."

Very frequently do we find the mind even in an enfeebled body, revealing unwonted vigor. Many famous names in art and in literature, in poetry and in philosophy, have been those whose merely physical powers were inferior, and who bore a heavy cross of sickness and of suffering. Coleridge in his *Table-Talk* remarks : "Illness never in the smallest degree affects my intellectual powers. I can *think* with all my ordinary vigor in the midst of pain ; . . . ." Extreme old age does not always reveal itself in failing intellect. Sometimes in the very article of death, sublimer thoughts are uttered than ever were conceived or expressed in the full vigor of life.

Quite in contrast with the teaching of Mr. Lawrence is the following from Prof. Jaumes, *Montpellier Médicale*, 1860 : "Thought, sentiment, will, do not imply any notion of number, of extent, of motion, and can, ought to, survive the body. . . . . A spirit is more than a creation of God, it is an emanation from God himself; it participates, doubtless in an inferior degree, but it participates in the Divine nature ; it is free, it loves, it knows itself and forms some conception of the Infinite Being from whom it came, and to whom it ought to return."

56. PAGE 109, LINE 13.

Ruskin.

57. PAGE 109, LINE 14.

Flourens.

58. PAGE 109, LINE 30.

Even Cabanis has said: "It is impossible for us to affirm that the dissolution of these organs involves that of this moral system."

Moreover, if the argument seems imperfectly presented, and I know that it is, let me request the doubter to read the page in Coleridge's Literary Remains, entitled Death and the Grounds of Belief in a Future State.

59. PAGE 110, LINE 8.

Even where no glory of sacrifice transforms the death-bed into an altar, our hearts would have us believe that he who breathes his last is only departing, not dying save as to his physical existence. Very truly has George MacDonald said, speaking for the moment from a purely materialistic side, *Paul Faber, Surgeon :* "What man can learn to look upon the dying as so much matter about to be rekneaded and remodelled into a fresh mass of feverous joys, futile aspirations, and stinging chagrins, without a self-contempt from which there is no shelter but the poor hope that we may be a little better than we appear to ourselves."

A few years ago the celebrated Pasteur, distributing prizes at the college he had been educated, in the course of his address, uttered these memorable words : " C'est insulter au coeur de l'homme que de dire avec le materialiste, la mort, c'est le neant !"

60. PAGE 110, LINE 16.

If the position here taken seems to any one unsound, let me remind the objector that it is similar to that of many eminent philosophical thinkers ; especially it is the same as that of Professor Acland, in the Harveian Oration* previously referred to.

"If physical science can put its fingers on nothing but a series of sequences, it merely proves that science is not philosophy, and is altogether a subordinate affair." (Prof. Blackie.) Indeed, in regarding the limitations of human knowledge, made by some writers upon science at the present day, one is reminded of the advice of the Geometer in Voltaire's *l'Homme aux* 40 *cens :* "I advise you to doubt everything, except that the three angles of a triangle are equal to two right angles, or that two triangles having the same base and the same height are equal, or similar propositions ; for example, two and two make four." This Geometer would have been a high priest in the temple of Agnosticism.

I cannot forbear quoting, in concluding this note, the following from an Oxford lecture delivered last year by Mr. Ruskin : "Of the dignity of physical science, and of the happiness of those who are devoted for the healing and the help of mankind, I never have meant to utter, and I do not think I have uttered one irreverent word. But against the curiosity of science, leading us to call virtually nothing gained but what is new discovery, and to despise every use of our knowledge in its acquisition; of the insolence of science, in claiming for itself a separate function of that human mind which, in its perfection, is one and indivisible in the image of its Creator, and of the perversion of science, in hoping to discover by the analysis of death what can only be discovered by the worship of life—of these I have spoken, not only with sorrow, but with a fear which every day I perceive to be more surely grounded, that such labor, in effacing from within you the sense of the presence of God in the garden of the earth, may awaken within you the prevailing echo of the first voice of its destroyer, ' Ye shall all be as gods.' "